How the Grinch Lusted after Santa

Helen Walton

Contents

A Short Story

♥

MY LIPS STILL TINGLED from the Grinch's mint-flavored kiss. I pressed a finger to my bottom lip to ease the sensation, and to stop the answer to Hazel's question about my feelings for the Grinch slipping out.

'It's the Most Wonderful Time of the Year' crooned through the speakers in the party room. It truly was my most wonderful time acting in the annual Christmas play in my hometown of Newberry, Australia.

Fellow actors clinked glasses full of spiked eggnog, still in costume, making the Christmas Eve after-party special. This year's play of 'How the Grinch Loved Christmas' was the best yet. Rave reviews poured in, fueling the director to add more rum to the eggnog in his delight.

Hazel tilted her head, sending the elf hat sliding over her eyes. She shoved it back and stared at me. "Well, Candy, tell me?"

"Well, what?" I smoothed the red velvet skirt of my Santa outfit. A twist in the play, a female Santa. I attempted to play it cool, but I didn't fool Hazel. She knew me too well.

Four years I'd lusted after the Grinch. Or more precisely, Devin Meyer, the ridiculously hot guy playing the Grinch. We'd shared a scorching on-stage kiss at the end of the play every Saturday night for six weeks, and every Friday night at rehearsals for six weeks before the play opened for the last four years. In those years, I'd wondered if he realized I didn't act when I kissed him for those twelve weeks. Four years I'd dreamed he felt the same way I did when his supple, yet demanding lips met mine.

Four years he'd been engaged. To someone else.

The unfairness of his commitment didn't stop me from kissing him on stage. The kiss was part of the show. Nor did his engagement stop the flood of desire coating my skin in an electrical current whenever he was near. The man was sexy and knew it. Devin's swagger drew looks from every female, young and old, with a small amount of drool. When he gazed at you with his dark, probing eyes and the half-smile of his supple lips, it was enough to make you want to rip off your panties and throw them at him.

It was a wonder he returned to Newberry to play the part of the Grinch. His stunning looks, excellent acting skills, and magnetic presence had him in high demand in Hollywood theaters. Unlike me, who still played bit parts in the smaller theaters. But I didn't mind, I loved my job, and the freedom to be anyone else once I slipped on the costume. For the last few months, I had the pleasure of being Santa to Devin's Grinch.

Hazel shot me a laser beam of annoyance from her eyes. It always amused me her eyes weren't hazel. Instead, they were deep blue.

"He's engaged," I reminded her.

"Are you sure? Your kiss tonight was spicier than last year." She raised a questioning eyebrow and shoved her elf hat back on her head. "I thought you two might tear each other's clothes off on stage."

I sighed, fantasizing about doing that very thing. Then huffed in annoyance. Our chemistry was enough to give me pause, but it was pointless. He was engaged.

Balthazar, the wise man, lurched in front of us with a glass of eggnog. He wrestled with his robe and tugged a sprig of greenery tied with a red bow from beneath the folds.

He hiccupped. "Kiss me, I've got mistletoe."

The wise man dangled the sprig over Hazel's head and leaned toward her with pursed lips. Hazel twisted her head. His mouth landed on her cheek with a loud, wet smack. Laughter bubbled from my chest and burst from my lips. The drunk fool missed his mark. He swung my way before I realized his intent and slipped his nutmeg-flavored tongue into my open mouth. I lifted my hands to shove him away, but he stumbled before I made contact.

The Grinch, aka Devin and Mr. Hotness himself, stood behind Balthazar, his hands on the wise man's shoulders.

"Hey, everyone," the wise man hollered, twisting out of Devin's hold. "Candy tastes like a candy cane."

He hooted at his joke, swigged more of his eggnog, which he didn't need, and staggered over to his next kiss victim.

"Somebody should stop him." I wiped my mouth with the back of my hand, hoping the next person saw him coming, and ran.

"I'll go knock him out," Devin said.

"No." I latched onto his arm and held him back. I couldn't let Devin punch a fellow actor and get kicked out of the play. Then I'd never see him again. Never kiss him again.

Devin dazzled me with his lopsided smile. I gazed at his lips in reverence. The man had amazing lips. Lips that kissed like... well, nothing I'd ever experienced. Or had since our first rehearsal kiss. Yep, panty throwing time.

His grin grew. "Candy, have you been drinking the eggnog too?"

I dragged my gaze away from his mouth. Only minutes or was it hours ago they'd been luring mine on one of our amazing stage kisses. "No, I don't like eggnog."

He leaned closer and whispered in my ear, "Me either."

His minty fresh breath breezed over my cheek. I breathed him in deep. If my skin wasn't already zinging with electricity, it would now. Peppermint. Every year Devin's kisses sent tingles to my lips with mint and him. After the first year, I'd chewed a peppermint before our kiss scene too. No wonder the wise man said I tasted like a candy cane.

"No boyfriend in the audience this year?"

He glanced at my hand on his arm. I let go of the firm hold I'd used to keep him with me.

"No." After last year's performance my then-boyfriend broke up with me spouting the kiss was too real, and I'd never kissed him like that. I couldn't deny it.

"So, you're single?"

"Yes, I have been all year." My cheeks warmed. *Why did I tell him that?* Mr. Hotness himself didn't want to hear about my lacking love life.

"Where's Tina?" I asked after his fiancée.

I scanned the overflowing party room decorated in an abundance of shining tinsel, twinkling colored lights, baubles, and bells. *Where did Hazel go?* She met my gaze from the other side of the room and raised her glass. How did I miss her moving away? Was I that enthralled by Devin?

"Tina's not here."

I snapped my gaze back to the sexiest Grinch ever. Devin dressed in green body paint and skin-tight leggings so he could perform his dance moves. And what moves he had. Along with a set of abs I wanted to run my hands over and rock-hard buttocks that mesmerized me whenever he turned.

"Where is she?"

She never missed the last performance or the big after-party on Christmas Eve.

"I don't know. We broke up last year."

My gaze left his green-covered chest to focus on his face. His half-smile tugged at the corner of his mouth, but I kept my gaze on his eyes. Hope flared with every resounding beat of my heart.

"I'm sorry," I said. It was something I should say, but my heart raced with the possibilities.

"Are you?" He dropped his gaze to my lips.

I dragged in an unsteady breath and released it on a heavy exhale with a puff. "No."

"Good." He took hold of my hands, which hung limp and lifeless after his announcement he was no longer engaged.

"Why did you break up?" I asked.

"After last year's show, she threw a hissy fit."

"What about?" It was hard to form a coherent thought with Devin holding my hands. *Did I dare think he liked me, too?*

"About our stage kiss."

"But it's acting," I argued for the sake of it. I'd never once acted when we kissed.

"Is it?"

I dragged in another breath filled with the exotic aroma of Devin. The one I looked forward to inhaling every year while he kissed me at rehearsals and on stage for the play. Mariah Carey's 'All I want for Christmas is You' drifted from the speakers. All I wanted for Christmas was Devin. This year I might have him for real if I was brave enough to admit my feelings.

I released my pent-up feelings on an exhale of longing. "No."

"All these years the kisses were real?"

"Every. Single. One."

"Candy, I've lusted after you since our first rehearsal. I didn't think...and I couldn't..."

"Me too, Devin." I sighed with relief. My four years of lusting weren't one-sided.

"So, Santa, what do you say? Would you like to date the Grinch?" He smiled his confident, lopsided grin. "You know how the Grinch loves Santa."

There was no resisting Devin when he smiled.

"Yes." I stepped closer. "Santa loves the Grinch too."

"I don't think we need mistletoe." He lowered his lips to mine.

"Never," I murmured against his lips.

Devin's demanding lips drew mine into a kiss to beat our earlier kisses. Off-stage and unquestionably real. This kiss was full of lust and the beginning of our mutual love. He was free to be mine. I was his. Had been for the last four years since the first time his supple lips branded mine. Every kiss between us would forever be genuine. No more pretending to act with my sexy Grinch.

I was in heaven as Devin's lips ravished mine.

Hazel hooted from across the party room, jolting me away from Devin. A glance around the room showed no one else noticed our off-stage lip lock. Our first genuine kiss. Every bit as hot and delicious as the kisses we shared on stage.

Devin swiped his tongue over his top lip as though tasting me again. "I'm heading back to my dressing room."

"Oh, okay." I deflated like a balloon after our real lust-filled kiss.

He ran his hands down my arms, over the soft velvet of my Santa dress, and threaded his fingers with mine. "Do you want to come with me? Help take the paint off my back?"

My blood raced through my body with an intense heat and threatened to make me pass out. Devin wanted me to touch him. He wanted me to turn him from the sexy Grinch into his true hotness.

Could I do it and not spontaneously orgasm?

"Okay," I said with a breathy exhale.

Releasing one hand, he pulled me through the crowd of Christmas costumed actors and toward his dressing room at the back of the theater. Hazel gave me a thumbs up on our way out of the party room, knocking her elf hat off in her enthusiasm. No one else noticed our departure. They were all too busy celebrating the success of the show with the spiked eggnog. Devin closed the thick door behind us, silencing the noise of the partygoers.

Alone together. Both single. And we'd admitted we lusted after the other. Possibly even had feelings for each other.

Devin gave me one of his lopsided panty melting smiles, lifted his hand, and traced my trembling lips. I flicked my tongue and licked his fingertip. His face filled with primal heat. I drew his finger into my mouth, wrapped my tongue around it, and sucked like I wanted to do to his cock.

He groaned. "All these years."

I released his finger and smiled with all the passion I held for him and him alone.

Devin pulled me flush against his firm body. I slid my arms up his bare back, reveling in the small shudder running through him at my touch. I wanted more. Touch. Kiss. Lick. Suck. All of it.

"Kiss me, Devin. Kiss me as us. Not the Grinch loving Santa and Santa loving the Grinch."

He met my challenge with more enthusiasm than our kisses had ever had. With no audience watching our kiss, we let our true desires rage against the other's mouth. Devin swept his tongue inside my mouth again and again. He claimed every inch as his. I let him. I was his. He was free to be mine. All mine and I wanted him. Every part of him.

I ran my hands down his smooth back. Devin let out a deep rumble in the back of his throat. Spurred on by our growing desires, I yanked at his skin-tight leggings and caressed my hands to the firm buttocks he'd flaunted in front of me for four years. Devin smoothed his hands up my sides and cupped my breasts. My nipples pebbled inside the velvet costume. I tugged his leggings down, wanting all of him. His erection sprang free from the tight confines of his pants. I dropped to my knees, wrapped my lips around his broad head, and drew him into the heat of my mouth.

"Candy," he growled, deep and throaty, before pulling back and joining me on the floor.

He slid his hands up my bare thighs, reached under my Santa skirt, and traced a finger over the front of my panties.

"Yes," I moaned.

He eased my panties to the side and found the slick wetness of my arousal. My head fell forward onto his chest. His touch was better than his kiss. He brushed my hair over my shoulder and trailed scorching kisses along my neck. I shifted, needing more. Devin's fingers teased the edge of my sensitive folds, driving me closer to the edge. But I wanted to come around him. With him.

"Devin." I sighed and grasped his arm.

"Sit on the Grinch's lap." He tilted my chin up.

I giggled. "Isn't it supposed to be the other way around? You're meant to sit on Santa's lap."

"Next time I'll dress as Santa." He eased a finger inside me.

My inner muscles rejoiced to have him buried deep.

"Condom in my wallet if you want to sit on the Grinch's lap."

He pressed deep, hitting a sweet spot. I struggled with my growing need to just let go and my deeper need to have him inside me and bring my dreams to life. With a push off the floor, I stood on quivering legs. Devin's wallet sat on the dressing table. I scooped it up and threw it at him. He grinned his lopsided sexy as sin smile, withdrew a condom, and rolled it on his hard length.

Hot. So hot.

He crooked a finger at me.

I stripped my panties, straddled his lap, and lowered myself onto him. His hard flesh met my welcoming folds. A full-body quiver ran through me at the intense pleasure of having Devin inside me. With me. Mine. His firm hands cupped my ass and eased me up and down his length. I'd forgotten everything in that moment of our first joining. His demanding lips met mine. I came to life, riding him and kissing him as though my life depended on this very moment with Devin.

Electricity raced across my skin in a tingling sensation and tunneled deep inside, sparking and building in power and intensity, until I gulped in Devin's peppermint breath. His kiss. His touch. All I'd ever wanted.

Needed. Reaching the point of no return, I cried out against his urgent lips. My hips clamped down on him. My orgasm ricocheted through my body with Devin buried deep inside. Moments later, his answering moan and pulsing release joined mine.

He placed gentle kisses around my face. I opened my lust and love haze-filled eyes. We'd smeared the green paint that covered his face and body into streaks across his face, chest and lower, across my Santa suit.

I now resembled a candy cane.

Devin chuckled. I giggled.

He tugged my Santa hat from my head. "That was a long time in the making."

I removed his Grinch hat and ran my fingers through his dark hair. "Mm-hmm." I couldn't form words after what we'd done. What this meant. I shifted on his lap.

He grasped my hips with his hands. "Where do you think you're going? You haven't told the Grinch what you want for Christmas yet."

An ecstatic grin tugged my lips until my cheeks hurt. "I don't need to. I just got it."

"Yeah?" He gave me one of his panty throwing grins.

If I was wearing panties, I'd give them to him.

"All I've ever wanted for Christmas was you."

He cupped my face and kissed me. This here, this was us. Everything we were and everything we'd become. Our kisses were our beginning and our future. A future with a lot of love by the feel of Devin hardening inside me. He rocked his hips. I gasped into his mouth.

"What?" he asked. "You didn't think I'd finished already after four years of kissing you."

"I guess my Christmas wish is coming true this year."

"Candy Kane, they're only just beginning." His dark eyes twinkled with lust, love, and a lot of mischief.

"Ugh," I groaned. "I wish my parents didn't name me that either."

"You never know what might happen next Christmas." Devin winked.

Next Christmas. Wishes. Dreams and our life together.

This Santa couldn't wait for next year's Grinch to lust after her and kiss her on stage. We had three hundred or so days to practice before our next show. I looked forward to every single day with my sexy Grinch Devin. No more waiting for the play to kiss Devin. Now I could do it any time I wanted.

I kissed him with love and lust. Let my four years of feelings free. Devin returned them all.

And then some.

Read Hazel and Valentine's story in Lusting After Valeintine the second short story in the Hollywood Hearts series.

Afterword

Thank you so much for reading How the Grinch Lusted after Santa. I hope you enjoyed this steamy short Christmas story.

Did you love my story?

Review it!

A reader who writes a review for a book is a tremendous gift to the author. It lets me know that someone read my book and enjoyed the story enough to tell me. If you enjoyed this book, please leave a review on Amazon or GoodReads. I'd be forever grateful.

Acknowledgments

First, thank you to my family for putting up with me disappearing into the world of books. A lot of work goes into creating a story, and I'm always thankful for the support of my online writing buddies, beta readers and fellow authors, Immy Moore for always making me smile, Tammy Petersen for believing in me from the start, Karen Lieversz for willing to read any level of heat I write. Also, my fabulous beta reader Erica Karwoski and your help with US English. The biggest thank you goes to my 'twin' Author Dannielle Line, who is the best critique partner, cheerleader, and sounding board ever, and is forever fixing my comma errors, sorry Dannielle I'm afraid you're stuck with them and me. Finally thank you to all you romance readers. You are my tribe.

About Author

Helen Walton is a tea drinking, chocoholic, romance writer. Stories are her obsession. She adores creating sensual romances containing a sprinkling of humor and the all-important happy ending. She lives in South Australia with her family, and menagerie of quirky animals where they all take her away from her book world and demand to be fed. Lucky for them, she enjoys cooking but prefers baking.

Sign up for my newsletter for exclusive content.

https://www.helenwaltonauthor.com/newsletter
Visit my website

https://www.helenwaltonauthor.com/

Follow me

a amazon.com/author/helenwalton

BB bookbub.com/profile/helen-walton

f facebook.com/Helen-Walton-Author-1034966677
06602/

g goodreads.com/author/show/20249188.Helen_W
alton

instagram.com/helen.walton.author

pinterest.com.au/HelenWaltonAuthor/boards/

tiktok.com/ZSJgrfgrC/

HOW THE GRINCH LUSTED AFTER SANTA

Also By

His Pleasure Contract

Love Negotiations

Her Love Submission

Hollywood Hearts Short Stories

How The Grinch Lusted After Santa

Lusting After Valentine

The Lustful Leprechaun

The Lust Bunny

Anthologies

Reluctant Bride

Alpha Male

www.ingramcontent.com/pod-product-compliance
Lightning Source LLC
Chambersburg PA
CBHW030419120726
47904CB00007B/2344